Great Expectations

Charles Dickens

Adapted by Richard Widdows

GALLERY BOOKS
An Imprint of W. H. Smith Publishers Inc.
112 Madison Avenue
New York City 10016

This book was devised and produced by
Multimedia Publications (UK) Ltd.

Editor: Richard Widdows (Acorn Press)
Designer: Janette Place
Production: Arnon Orbach

First published in the United States of America 1985 by
Gallery Books, an imprint of W. H. Smith Publishers Inc.,
112 Madison Avenue, New York, NY 10016

ISBN 0 8317 4009 4

Typeset by Waveney Typesetters, Norwich, Norfolk
Origination by DS Colour International Ltd., London
Printed in Italy by Amilcare Pizzi SpA., Milan

Contents

The Life of Charles Dickens

Charles John Huffham Dickens was born on 7 February 1812, in the English coastal town of Portsmouth, where his father, John Dickens, was a clerk in the Navy Pay Office. John Dickens was 26 when Charles was born and was an excitable, extravagant man who liked to entertain in style — a style that his meagre salary as a clerk was unable to support. This was to lead him into a succession of financial crises throughout his life.

The second of eight children, Charles was a delicate, sensitive child, unable to join in the play of other children, and he withdrew into books. Later in life, recalling his boyhood days, he wrote: "When I think of it, the picture always arises in my mind of a summer evening, the boys at play in the churchyard and I sitting on my bed, reading as if for life."

The books that he read, introduced to him by his father — books such as *Robinson Crusoe*, *The Arabian Nights*, *Don Quixote* and a child's *Tom Jones* — created for him a world of magic, wonder and adventure, a world that he himself was so vividly to create for others to enjoy in his own books.

At the age of 12 the childhood of Dickens came to a sudden and dramatic end. His father, unable to pay his large debts, was packed off to the Marshalsea Debtors' Prison in London. Within a few days the rest of the family were to join him there — all, that is, except Charles, whose education was cut short and who was made to earn his living, washing bottles, at Warren's Blacking Factory. This experience proved so shocking and humiliating to the boy that it was to haunt him for the rest of his life. "No words can express the secret agony of my soul . . . I felt my early hopes of growing up to be a learned and distinguished man crushed in my breast."

Though soon re-united with his family, the previous easy life enjoyed by Charles was never to return. Two years later, at the age of 14, his irregular and inadequate schooling ended and he began work as a clerk in a lawyer's office in Gray's Inn, London. This experience, again not a happy one, gave him two things — a lifelong loathing of the legal profession and much raw material for many of his later novels.

Dickens then became a reporter on the parliamentary newspaper *True Sun*, where his natural talent for reporting and keen observation was first recognized. He taught himself shorthand and, on the *Mirror of Parliament*, and then the *Morning Chronicle*, he was soon acknowledged as the best parliamentary reporter of the age.

In 1833, now very much the young man about town, Dickens wrote his first piece of fiction: *A Dinner at Poplar Walk*, in the *Old Monthly Magazine*. Asked by the editor to contribute more, under the pen name 'Boz', Dickens wrote a series of pieces that were collected and published in 1836 under the title *Sketches by Boz*.

The modest success of *Sketches* was followed by the enormously popular and successful *Pickwick Papers*, which was published in monthly instalments in 1836 and 1837. Pickwick became a national hero overnight, and his exploits were followed by an average of 40,000 readers. Though not yet 30, Dickens was now rich and famous.

Two days after the publication of Pickwick, Dickens married Catherine Hogarth, daughter of a fellow journalist. "So perfect a creature never breathed," he wrote of her at the time, "she had not a fault." But with time his view of her was to change, and in later years he was to admit, "She is amiable and complying but nothing on earth would make her understand me." They were to separate in 1858, when Dickens was 46.

Throughout his life Dickens enjoyed travelling. In the 1840s he journeyed to Scotland, America, France, Switzerland and Italy. And throughout this period he poured out a succession of novels that exposed the cruelty, hypocrisy and appalling poverty of early Victorian society, novels such as *Oliver Twist*, *Nicholas Nickleby*, *The Old Curiosity Shop*, *Barnaby Rudge*, *A Christmas Carol*, *Martin Chuzzlewit*, and *Dombey and Son*.

Even his novel writing (which continued to be published in monthly instalments) proved inadequate for his boundless energy and restless spirit. In the 1840s, apart from all his major novels, and work on *David Copperfield* (published in 1850), he started a daily newspaper, the *Daily News*, and a weekly magazine, *Household Words*, in addition to writing a travel book *American Notes* and a three-volume *Child's History of England*.

In all that he wrote Dickens strove to draw people together and lead them to a better understanding of each other. As he himself believed, "In this world a great deal of bitterness among us arises from an imperfect understanding of one another."

But as he grew older, the subjects he wrote of grew bleaker and the mood more grim. *Bleak House, Hard Times, Little Dorrit, A Tale of Two Cities, Great Expectations, Our Mutual Friend* and his unfinished novel, *The Mystery of Edwin Drood*, all reflect a growing pessimism.

Despite a steady decline in health, Dickens continued to give dramatic public readings of his works to packed houses in both Britain and the United States, which he visited again in 1867–68. Of these a contemporary witness reported, "He seemed to be physically transformed as he passed from one character to another; he had as many distinct voices as his books had characters; he held at command the fountains of laughter and tears . . . When he sat down it was not mere applause that followed, but a passionate outburst of love for the man."

But the strain proved too much and on 8 June 1870, during a farewell series of talks in England, he suffered a stroke, and the next day he died at his home, Gad's Hill Place, near Rochester, Kent, at the age of 58.

Two days after his death Queen Victoria wrote in her diary, "He is a very great loss. He had a large loving mind and the strongest sympathy with the poorer classes." On 14 June he was buried in Poet's Corner, Westminster Abbey, close to the monuments of Chaucer and Shakespeare.

Charles Dickens in his study at Gad's Hill Place, his home near Rochester, Kent, reproduced by kind permission of the Trustees of the Dickens House (*Dickens' Dream* by R. W. Buss)

Introduction

SEVERAL of Dickens' novels are about "great expectations" since they have as their central theme the rags-to-riches story of a poor, underprivileged boy who is finally accepted into polite society. It is strange then, given the happy endings of both *Oliver Twist* and *David Copperfield*, that *Great Expectations* ends with the main character, Pip, being stripped of his wealth and his position in society.

Unlike *Oliver Twist* and *David Copperfield*, whom we come to like and even admire, Pip is not really a hero. Despite his virtues, he becomes a snob and is corrupted by his good fortune. Suddenly removed from his labours in a country smithy and sent to London to be educated as a gentleman, he is impressed by the wrong people for the wrong reasons. He neglects and abandons the honest, hardworking folk who have always cared for him, he is irritated and embarrassed by the gentle blacksmith Joe Gargery, and his pride is hurt when he learns who his mysterious benefactor is.

But Pip's snobbery is not blind or callous; he is aware of it and often expresses guilt for his behaviour. In the end his feelings for the convict Magwitch are our own: fear of his violent nature and a dislike of his crude ways, but admiration for his courage.

For many years Pip is kept in ignorance of his benefactor. Is it the frightening Miss Havisham, deserted on her wedding day and living in a mansion of memories and cobwebs? Is it the sinister Mr Jaggers, the lawyer who pays Pip his generous allowance? And for years Pip nurses a fascination for the icy and beautiful Estella, trained by Miss Havisham to "break men's hearts". Perhaps because his good fortune has come to him so easily, Pip is not a man who makes many friends, apart that is from the cheerful Herbert Pocket.

Written in 1860 and 1861, in the twilight of his life, *Great Expectations* was the thirteenth of Dickens' fourteen major novels, and it marked a return to more familiar territory after his excursions abroad in *A Tale of Two Cities*. From the very start — it has the most dramatic and gripping start of all Dickens' novels — it unfolds a story that drives eagerly forward, full of emotion and humour, and full — as always in Dickens — of unforgettable characters.

1 Strange Encounters

My father's surname being Pirrip, and my Christian name being Philip, I could make little of either when I was very young except 'Pip'. So I called myself Pip, and came to be called Pip.

I give Pirrip as my family name on the authority of my father's tombstone and that of my sister, Mrs Joe Gargery, who married the blacksmith. As I never saw my father or mother, nor a picture of them, my first impressions were inspired by their tombstone. The shape of the letters gave me the idea that my father was a square, stout man; and from the inscription *'Also Georgina, Wife of the Above'*, I drew the conclusion that my mother was freckled and sickly. Next to their grave were five stone tablets, each about a foot and a half long, sacred to the memory of five brothers of mine, all of whom gave up the struggle for life before they had reached an age to talk.

The bleak churchyard holding the graves was set on a low hill in the wilderness of the marsh country where I lived — flat country intersected with dykes and mounds and ditches. Beyond it was the winding river, and beyond that, some twenty miles away, was the sea.

As I knelt before my parents' grave on that raw afternoon, towards evening on Christmas Eve, I suddenly felt more alone and more helpless than I had ever felt before in my life, and I began to cry.

"Hold your noise!" cried a terrible voice. "Keep still, you little devil, or I'll cut your throat!"

Next to me there was now a fearful man, all in coarse brown, with irons round his legs; a man who limped and shivered, and glared and growled, and whose teeth chattered in his head as he seized me with his great hands.

"Don't cut my throat, sir!" I pleaded in terror, my face only inches from his. "Please don't, sir!"

"Tell us your name, boy! Quick!"

"Pip, sir!"

"Show us where you live. Point out the place!"

"Over there, sir," I said, pointing to our village. "About a mile away."

"Where's your mother?"

"There, sir. She's in her grave. And my father."

"Who do you live with, then — supposing you're let to live, which I ain't made up my mind about?"

"My sister, sir — Mrs Joe Gargery — wife of the blacksmith."

"Blacksmith, eh?"

The man looked down at the irons on his legs,

then back at me, and then took me by both arms and tilted me back on a tombstone.

"Now look'ee here. You know what a file is?"

"Yes, sir."

"Well you get me a file, and you get me some victuals. And you bring 'em to me here, early tomorrow morning. You do it, and you never dare say a word to no-one, or I'll have your heart and liver. Now, be off!"

He let go of me suddenly. Then I ran out of the graveyard, down the hill to the road and all the way home without stopping.

Home was a wooden house, with Joe's stone forge joined to it. He was a simple, good-natured, sweet-tempered, easy-going fellow, and I always treated him as a larger kind of child, and as no more than my equal.

My sister was more than twenty years older than I, and had established a great reputation with herself and the neighbours because she had brought me up 'by hand'. Having at that time yet to find out what the expression meant, and knowing her to have a hard and heavy hand, and

to be as much in the habit of laying it on her husband as on me, I supposed that Joe Gargery and I were both brought up 'by hand'.

She was not a good-looking woman, my sister. She was tall and scraggy, and I had the general impression that she must have made Joe marry her 'by hand'.

When I entered the house that cold afternoon, my heart racing with the thought of the task before me, Joe was at the table and my sister was cooking supper. She turned and waved her great ladle at me.

"There you are, you beast of a boy! You'll wear me out with fret and worry, you will. Where have you been?"

"I've — I've been to the churchyard."

"To the churchyard!" repeated my sister, grabbing me by the ear and dumping me on my stool. "If it weren't for me you'd have been to the churchyard long ago, and stayed there under a stone. Who brought you up by hand?"

"You did."

"And why did I do it, I should like to know? I'd never do it again, I know that. I may truly say

I've not had this apron off since you were born. It's bad enough to be a blacksmith's wife, without being your mother!"

Though I was hungry, I dared not eat my hunk of bread and butter, since I knew Mrs Joe was a strict housekeeper and I may find little food available later. So I took advantage of Joe's going to poke the fire to slip the bread under my shirt.

When he sat down again, Joe looked at me in wonder.

"You'll do yourself a mischief, Pip, old chap. It'll stick somewhere. You can't have chewed it!"

"Been bolting his food, has he?" cried my sister, pulling me up by the hair. "You come along and be dosed."

Mrs Joe always kept a supply of tar-water in the cupboard, and at the best of times so much of the mixture was administered to me that I was conscious of going round smelling like a new fence. But the urgency of this occasion demanded a pint of the mixture, poured down my throat while Mrs Joe held my head under her arm. Joe was made to swallow half a pint because 'he had had a turn'; I should say he certainly had a turn afterwards, if he had not had one before.

I was warming myself by the fire before going to bed, when there was the sound of a great gun being fired.

"There's another convict off!" said Joe.

"What does that mean?" I asked.

"Escaped!" said my sister. "Escaped!"

"There was a convict off last night after sunset-gun," explained Joe. "And they fired warning of him. And now it seems they're firing warning of another."

"Who's firing."

"Drat the boy!" interposed my sister. "Ask no questions and you'll be told no lies."

My curiosity, spurred by the meeting at the churchyard, made me far braver than usual.

"Mrs Joe, I should very much like to know where the firing comes from."

"Lord bless the boy!" exclaimed my sister, meaning the very opposite. "From the hulks!"

"Please — what's the hulks?"

"That's the way with this boy! Answer him a question and he'll ask you a dozen more. Hulks are prison-ships, moored across the marshes."

"I wonder who's put into prison-ships, and why they're put there," I said.

My last query seemed too much for Mrs Joe, and she hovered over me, glaring. "People are put into hulks because they murder, and rob, and forge, and do all sorts of bad; and they always begin by asking questions. Now, get along to bed!"

I slept little, fearing now that the hulks were also for me: I had begun by asking questions, after all, and I was going to rob Mrs Joe! But the threat of the man with the irons on his leg seemed even greater, and as soon as daylight appeared at my window the next morning, I sneaked downstairs.

The pantry was far better supplied than usual, owing to Christmas, and I took a piece of cheese,

half a jar of mincemeat, some brandy from a stone bottle and a handsome pork pie.

There was a door from the kitchen into Joe's forge. I unbolted it, and found a file among his tools. I put it under my belt and made off across the misty marshes.

to take some of the liquor. He shivered violently all the while, and it was as much as he could do to keep the bottle between his teeth.

He was soon eating everything at once, like a hungry dog, but breaking off now and again to stop and look around him and listen to the wind.

"Brought anyone with you, boy?"

"No, sir! I swear it!"

He carried on devouring the food, wasting some in his haste, when I timidly asked him if he was going to leave any for the other one.

"Other one? What other one?"

"The other convict. He was here, just now."

"What did he look like?" he said, standing up.

"His face was hurt, sir, on his cheek."

"Where is he? Show me the way he went! I'll pull him down like a bloodhound!"

He tried to move in the direction I was pointing, but the irons brought him down.

"Curse these irons! Give me the file, boy. Quick!"

I handed him the file and in a moment he was working at the chain between the cuffs.

"I'll hunt him down. I'll hunt that gentleman down and feed him to the dogs. I'll get him before they get me! Compeyson! I'm coming after you — you hear me? I'll get you!"

I told him I must go, but he took no notice, so I slipped away. The last I saw of him, his head was bent over his knees and he was working in a frenzy at his fetter; the last I heard of him, when I stopped at the bottom of the hill, he was still shouting curses at the chain and his bleeding legs, and the file was still going.

It was not yet full light when I reached the churchyard, but I could make out a figure sitting on the first tombstone, his back towards me, and nodding forward as if asleep. I went up and touched him on the shoulder. He jumped up and spun round! It was not the same man, but another!

Yet this man was dressed in coarse brown, too, and was everything the other was, except that he was thinner and had a scar on his face. He swore an oath at me, made a lunge at me, missed — and stumbled out of the churchyard and away down the hill to the marshes.

I had gone only a few more paces when the other man appeared — hugging himself and limping, his body shaking with cold and his face pale with hunger.

"What's in the bottle, boy?"

"Brandy."

He was already eating the bread, and stopped

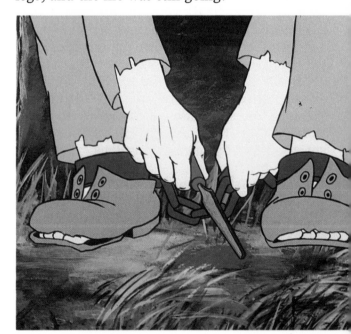

I fully expected to find a constable in the kitchen when I returned. But not only was there no officer; no discovery had yet been made of the theft. Mrs Joe was busy getting the house ready for the day, and when I walked in she was vigorously sweeping the floor.

"And where the deuce have you been?" was her seasonal greeting to me.

"Merry Christmas, Mrs Joe," I replied. "I've been down to the village to hear the carols."

"Carols, is it? Well, you might have done worse. Perhaps if I weren't a slave with her apron never off, I should have been to hear them. I'm rather partial to carols myself."

My sister having so much to do, Joe and I were then ordered to clean up, get changed and go off to church, before coming back for our Christmas dinner.

We were to have a superb meal of leg of pickled pork and greens and a roast stuffed fowl, followed by mince pie and pudding. The table was to be blessed, as usual, with the presence of Uncle Pumblechook. He was Joe's uncle, a well-to-do corn chandler in the nearest town who drove his own smart chaise-cart, and he always brought wine and money on Christmas Day. He was a plump, hard-breathing man, with a mouth like a fish, and an appetite to match his girth. After the pudding Mrs Joe asked him if he had had enough to eat.

"After such a feast, madam, I doubt if I shall break bread until the New Year!"

"Oh, that's a shame then, Uncle Pumblechook. I laid aside a pork pie, especially for you."

"Well! In that case it would be impolite of me to refuse. Just a small piece, mind."

I held tight to the table leg, awaiting the discovery, as my sister went to the pantry. After an age she came back, her face reddening. "The pie — it's gone! The pie's *gone!*"

"Gone?" repeated Uncle Pumblechook. "Gone?"

My sister glared at me, her hands on her hips, and I knew the game was up. I stood, prepared for the worst, when there was a noise outside the house and a loud knock on the door. I was only too happy to take advantage, and ran to open it. It was a sergeant of the army, and in his hand he held a pair of handcuffs.

15

"Excuse me for interrupting on such a day," he said, putting a hand on my shoulder, "but I am on a chase in the name of the King, and I need the blacksmith."

"I'm the blacksmith," said Joe proudly. "What's the trouble, sergeant?"

"We've had an accident with these cuffs, and the coupling ain't working. Could you cast your eyes over 'em — they're wanted for immediate service."

Joe looked at them and said the repair would take an hour or so; then, aided by me, he set to work. In just under an hour — during which time both hosts and visitors drank several glasses of the wine brought by Uncle Pumblechook — the roaring and the ringing in the forge stopped, and the soldiers prepared to leave.

The sergeant suggested to Joe that he might like to go along, and take me with him. Joe asked my sister and, to my great surprise, she agreed, but with one parting shot: "If you bring the boy back with his head blown to bits by a musket, don't look to me to put it together again!"

So off we set, and when we were out in the cold air and moving on, I whispered to Joe: "I hope we shan't find them, Joe!" And he whispered to me: "Pip, old chap, I'd give a shilling if they have cut and run!"

We went first to the churchyard, which was searched, and then struck out across the marshes. Now we were in the wilderness I considered for the first time whether, if we should come upon them, my convict would

suppose it was I who had brought the soldiers to him.

Suddenly we all heard noises, shouting a fair way off — at least two voices. Then we heard a soldier yell, "There they are, the both of 'em!"; and we ran behind the sergeant to the top of the mound. Below him, in the mire, the two convicts were fighting like wild beasts. The sergeant pointed his gun in the air and fired.

"Surrender, you two! Come asunder!"

The two prisoners struggled to their feet, panting and bleeding.

"Mind this!" said my convict. "I took him. I give him up to you!"

"It'll do you little good," said the sergeant, "being in the same plight. Handcuffs there!"

"I don't expect it to do me any good. I took him and he knows it. That's good enough for me."

"He tried to — to murder me!" gasped the other one. "You bear witness!"

"Look'ee here!" said my convict to the sergeant. "Single-handed I got clear of the ship. And I would have got clear of these death-cold flats if I hadn't made the discovery that he was here. Let him go free? Oh no! I held him in that

grip that you could find him safe."

"Enough of this!" snapped the sergeant. "It's getting dark. Light them torches!"

As the torches were being prepared, my convict turned and saw me. He gave me a look I did not understand, but it all passed in a moment, and he never looked at me again.

"All right!" shouted the sergeant. "March!"

"Hold up," said my convict. "There's something I want to say. It may stop some persons being suspected because of me."

"You can say what you like," replied the sergeant, "but you've no call to say it here, in this forsaken place. You'll have opportunity enough before it's all done with, you know that."

"But this is a separate matter. A man can't starve — at least I can't. I took some victuals, up at the village over yonder, near where the church stands out of the marshes."

"You mean *stole*," said the sergeant.

"Yeah, stole. From the blacksmith's."

"Hallo!" said the sergeant, staring at Joe.

"Hallo," said Joe, staring at me.

"It was some broken victuals, and a dram of liquor, and a pie. That's what it was."

"Have you happened to miss such an article as a pie, blacksmith?" asked the sergeant.

"My wife did, didn't she, Pip?"

"So you're the blacksmith, are you?" said the convict, turning his eyes on Joe, but without the least glance at me. "Then I'm sorry that I ate your pie."

"God knows you're welcome to it," returned Joe, "so far as it was ever mine. We don't know what you've done wrong, but we wouldn't have you starved to death for it, a poor fellow creature. Would us, Pip?"

As I shook my head in silent agreement the procession began its journey back to the prison-ship, with Joe and I at the rear. Soon I could walk no more, and the last thing I remember of that strange, sad day was climbing on to Joe's broad back as we parted ways from the soldiers and their miserable captives.

2 Satis House

I do not recall feeling guilty towards Mrs Joe when the fear of being found out was lifted off me. But I loved Joe — perhaps for no better reason than because the dear fellow let me love him — and I thought that I should tell him the whole truth, particularly when I first saw him looking about for his lost file. Yet I did not, for the fear of losing Joe's confidence, of losing my companion and friend, tied up my tongue.

Life all too quickly returned to normal after Christmas and the excitement of the convicts. When I was old enough I was to be apprenticed to Joe, and in the meantime my schooling consisted of an hour each evening in the room above the general shop of the village.

Our teacher was the great aunt of Mr Wopsle, a friend of my sister's and a clerk of the church,

and she had an orphaned grand-daughter called Biddy. Though only the same age as me, Biddy all but ran the shop for her grandmother as far as I could make out, and she was very clever. It was partly because of Biddy's help, as well as my own efforts, that I struggled through the alphabet as if it had been a bramble-bush, getting scratched by every letter, and learned my tables.

I could expect no help from Joe, since his blacksmith father — a drunkard who used to beat both Joe and his mother horribly — had never allowed him to learn. Joe told me all about his wretched childhood one evening around this time, when he had been impressed by my progress at writing, and I loved him all the more after hearing it.

The day after this talk, I was told by my sister that Uncle Pumblechook wished to speak to me in the sitting-room on a matter of importance.

"You have heard of Miss Havisham, Pip?" he asked, as he stood by the window.

"Yes, sir." Everybody had heard of Miss Havisham as an immensely rich and grim lady who lived a life of seclusion in a large house.

"Miss Havisham is a lady of considerable wealth, and she has sought my advice. 'Mr Pumblechook,' says she, 'do you know of any boy who would be able to come here and play?' 'I do, ma'am,' I replied, 'and his name is Pip.' "

"So that's where you're going," said my sister. "You're to go to town with Uncle Pumblechook

ablutions were completed, I was handed over to Mr Pumblechook, who formally received me as if he were the sheriff. "Be forever grateful to all friends, boy," he said gravely, "but especially unto them that brought you up by hand!"

Joe, who appeared to be as confused by all the activity as I was, came out to see me off. "You'd best do as they say, Pip. God bless you, old chap."

"Goodbye, Joe!"

I had never been parted from him before, and I was confused, wondering why on earth I was going to play at Miss Havisham's, and what on earth I was expected to play at.

this evening, and he'll take you with his own hands to Miss Havisham's house in the morning. Your fortune could be made by this, so you mind your manners!"

With that she pounced on me, like an eagle on a lamb, and my face was squeezed into sinks, and my head was put under taps, and I was soaped, and kneaded, and rasped and towelled until I was almost beside myself. When these

We set out in the cart the next morning at ten o'clock, the short journey being taken up — as the dreary breakfast had been — with a series of sums asked by Mr Pumblechook.

Miss Havisham's house was vast and dismal, with many iron bars in it, and some of the windows bricked up. The gate to the courtyard was locked, so we had to wait until someone came to open it. As we waited I noticed that the clock on the tower of the old disused brewery was stopped on twenty minutes to nine o'clock.

"What name?" said a young voice from the

other side of the gate.

"Pumblechook."

"Quite right," said the voice, and the gate was opened. The owner of the voice was a young lady, who was very pretty and seemed very proud.

"This," said Mr Pumblechook, "is Pip."

"This is Pip, is it? Well come in, Pip."

Mr Pumblechook made to come in too, but the girl stopped him with the gate. "Oh! Do you wish to see Miss Havisham?"

"If Miss Havisham wishes to see me," replied Mr Pumblechook.

"Ah, but you see — she don't!"

This was said so finally that Mr Pumblechook raised no protest. But he was severely ruffled, and departed with the words: "Boy! Let your behaviour here be a credit upon them that brought you up by hand!"

My young guide locked the gate and led me across the courtyard. I stopped to look at the old brewery that was at the side of the house, now empty and decaying, and then up at the inscription on the main door: 'Satis House'.

"Where does the name come from, miss?"

"It's Greek, or Latin, or Hebrew, or all three for 'enough'."

"Enough House! That's a curious name, miss."

"It meant, when it was given, that whoever had this house could want for nothing else. They must have been easily satisfied in those days, I should think. But come on now, boy. Don't loiter!"

Though she called me 'boy' she was only a little older than myself. She seemed a good deal older, of course, being a girl and beautiful and self-possessed; and she was as scornful of me as if she had been twenty-one, and a queen.

We went into the house by a side door — the great front entrance had two chains across it — and the first thing I noticed was that the passages were all dark. She picked up a lighted candle, and we went through more passages and up a huge staircase, until at last we came to a door.

"Go in," she said.

"After you, miss."

"Don't be ridiculous, boy. *I'm* not going in." And she walked away, taking the candle with her.

lace, and silks — all of faded white. She had not quite finished dressing, and her bright jewels and trinkets lay on her table beside the looking-glass.

"Who is it?" said the lady.

"Pip, ma'am."

"Pip?"

"Mr Pumblechook's boy, ma'am. Come, to play."

"Come nearer. Let me look at you. Come closer."

It was when I stood before her that I could see that her face was white too, and saw all the objects around her in detail. I noticed that a clock in the room had also stopped at twenty minutes to nine.

"Look at me," said Miss Havisham. "You're not afraid of a woman who has never seen the sun since before you were born?"

"No," I lied.

"Do you know what I touch here," she said, laying her right hand on her left side.

"Your heart, ma'am?"

"Broken!"

She laid great emphasis on the word, and kept her hand there for some time. "Oh, I'm tired. I

After a moment I knocked, and was told from within to enter. I went in and found myself in a large room, well lit with wax candles, but no glimpse of daylight could be seen. Everything in the room — furniture, curtains, scattered clothes — was old and musty.

On a chair by the dressing-table sat the strangest lady I have ever seen, or will ever see. She was dressed in rich materials — satins, and

want diversion, and I've done with men and women. Now play. Play!"

I cannot think of an order in the world more difficult to obey; indeed I felt almost incapable of any movement at all.

"Are you sullen and obstinate?"

"No, ma'am, but I can't just — play. If you complain of me I shall get into trouble with my sister, so I would do it if I could. But it's so new here, and so strange, and so sad —"

I stopped, fearing I might say too much, or for that matter, had done so already.

She turned her eyes from me, and took up her looking-glass, and gazed into it. "So new to him," she muttered, "so old to me; so strange to him, so familiar to me; and so sad to both of us. Call Estella."

As she was still looking at herself, I thought she was still talking to herself.

"Call Estella!" she repeated, flashing a hard look at me. "You can do that! Call Estella!"

To stand in the dark in a mysterious passage of an unknown house, bawling Estella to a scornful young lady, and feeling it a liberty to speak her name at all, was almost as bad as trying to play to order.

But she answered at last and stood before Miss Havisham, who was now sitting at a small table in the middle of the room.

"My dear, let me see you play cards with this boy."

"With *him*? But he is a common labouring-boy!"

I thought I heard Miss Havisham's answer as she leaned towards the girl, only it seemed so unlikely: "Well! You can break his heart!"

"What do you play, boy?" asked Estella, sitting down.

"Nothing but beggar my neighbour, miss."

"Beggar him, Estella," said Miss Havisham, and we sat down to play cards.

"He calls the knaves Jacks, this boy!" cried Estella before our first game was finished. "And what coarse hands he has!"

I had never thought of being ashamed of my hands before, but I was now. Her contempt for me was so strong that it became infectious, and I caught it.

She won the game, and I dealt. That is, I misdealt, and she denounced me for being a stupid, clumsy labouring-boy.

"You say nothing of her," remarked Miss Havisham to me as she looked on. "She says many hard things of you, yet you say nothing of her. What do you think of her?"

"I — I don't like to say."

"Tell me in my ear," said Miss Havisham, bending down and leaning towards me.

"I think she's very proud," I whispered.

"Anything else?"

"I think she's very pretty."

"Anything else?"

"I think she's very insulting."

"Anything else?"

"I think I should like to go home."

"And never see her again, though she is so pretty?"

"I should like to see her again, but I should like to go home now."

Miss Havisham straightened in her chair. "You shall go soon," she said aloud. "Play the game out."

place to hide my face, and slipped down to the brewery wall, and cried. And as I cried I kicked the wall, trying to get rid of my injured feelings. In a while I returned, and the food and the beer made me feel a little better.

After a quarter of an hour or so Estella came down, carrying the keys, and touched me with a taunting hand.

"Why don't you cry," she said.

"Because I don't want to."

"You do. You've been crying till you are half blind, and you are near crying again now."

She laughed, and unlocked the gate, and let me out. I went straight to Mr Pumblechook's, and was relieved to find him out. So, leaving word in his shop that I was wanted at Miss Havisham's the following Tuesday, I set off on the four-mile walk to the forge. I pondered as I went along on all that I had seen, and thought that I was much more common and ignorant than I had ever considered myself until that morning.

I played the game to an end with Estella, and she won again. Then she threw the cards down on the table, as if she despised them for being won off me.

"When shall I have you here again?" said Miss Havisham. "Let me think."

I was beginning to remind her that it was Wednesday when she checked me with an impatient movement of her right hand.

"I know nothing of days of the week; I know nothing of weeks of the year. Come again after six days. Do you hear?"

"Yes, ma'am."

"Estella, take him down. Let him have something to eat and drink, and he can roam about if he wants before he leaves. Now go, Pip."

I followed the candle down, as I had followed it up, and when I finally came into the daylight I felt as if I had been in that room for many hours.

Estella left me in the courtyard and returned a few minutes later with some bread and meat and a small mug of beer. She put it down on the ground, as though I were a dog in disgrace, and I was so hurt that tears started to my eyes. The moment they sprang there the girl looked at me with a delight in having been the cause of them. Then, with a contemptuous toss of the head, she left me.

When she was gone, I looked about me for a

When I reached home my sister was very curious to know all about Miss Havisham's, and I soon found myself being cuffed about because my

answers were not thought long enough. The worst of it was that Mr Pumblechook came over at tea-time to have the details given to him, and his manner and nosiness made me keep my answers even shorter.

When Mr Pumblechook asked me what Miss Havisham was like, and I replied 'tall, thin and dark', and he replied 'Good!', I realized that he had never set eyes on the lady, and I could not then stop myself playing games on them. I told them that Miss Havisham sat in a black velvet sedan-chair in her room, that we ate cake off gold plates and drank wine out of goblets, and that Estella and I played with flags and swords.

If they had asked any more questions I think I would have betrayed myself, but then Joe came in for his tea and my sister insisted on relating my tales to him. While she and Mr Pumblechook sat debating whether I would be rewarded with property or money or both as a result of my visits, Joe was sent back to the forge by his wife for daring to suggest that I may receive nothing at all.

After Mr Pumblechook had driven off, I stole into the forge to Joe, and remained by him until he had finished for the night.

"Before the fire goes out, Joe, I should like to tell you something."

"Should you, Pip? Then tell us."

"About Miss Havisham's, Joe — it isn't true."

"You don't mean to say it's lies, Pip?"

"Yes, all of it. Terrible, isn't it?"

"Terrible? That it is, Pip. What possessed you?"

"I don't know, Joe. I don't know. It just happened."

I told Joe that I was very miserable, that I hadn't been able to explain myself to Mrs Joe and Mr Pumblechook, that there had been a beautiful girl at Miss Havisham's who was so proud, and that she had said I was common, and that I knew I was common, and that the lies had come out of it somehow, but I didn't know how.

"There's one thing you can be sure of, Pip," said Joe after some thought. "Namely, that lies is lies. However they come, they didn't ought to come. Don't you tell no more of 'em, Pip. That ain't the way to get out of being common, old chap. As to being common, I can't make it out —

you're an uncommon scholar."

"I've learned next to nothing, Joe. You think a lot of me, that's all."

"Well, Pip, you must be a common scholar afore you can be an uncommon one. The king upon his throne can't write his acts of parliament without having begun by learning his alphabet, though I can't say I've exactly done it."

I was touched by Joe's words, and asked him if we was angry with me.

"No, Pip, I ain't. But bearing in mind what you've done, you'd better drop it into your prayers when you go upstairs to bed. That's all, old chap, and don't never do it no more!"

I did include it in my prayers, but I wasn't long in bed before I began thinking how common Estella would consider Joe, and how coarse his hands, and how crude his ways.

3 I Become an Apprentice

It struck me next morning that the best step I could take towards making myself more uncommon was to get out of Biddy everything she knew — and it happened that on Thursday, after delivering groceries to a neighbour, she would always collect me at my house on the way to her grandmother's class.

"Biddy," I said cautiously before we set out for the village, "I know that you're more learned than me . . ."

"Than *I*, Pip," she laughed. "Than *I*!"

"— that you're more learned than I. But, well, could you teach me?"

"Of course, Pip, whenever I can. But I'm not that much of a scholar."

She may not have been the most beautiful girl in the world, Biddy Worple, but she was certainly the most obliging. She began her instruction right then, on the walk to the village, and by the time I arrived at Miss Havisham's the following week I firmly believed I had made some considerable progress in the knowledge of things.

As before, Estella locked the gate after admitting me to Satis House, and led me across the courtyard. When we reached the middle she suddenly stopped, and put her face quite close to mine: "Well?"

"Well, miss," I answered, almost bumping into her.

"Am I pretty?"

"Yes, I think you're very pretty."

"And am I insulting?"

"Not as much as you were last time."

"Not as much?"

"No."

She then kicked me on the shin as hard as she could, and I clutched my leg in pain.

"What do you think of me now, you coarse little monster?"

"I won't tell you."

"You're going to tell upstairs — is that it?"

"No, that's not it at all."

"Why don't you cry, you little wretch?"

"Because I'll never cry for you again," I said — which was, I suppose, as false a declaration as was ever made.

Just then I heard a deep voice behind me, from near the barred window.

"And whom have we here?"

The voice belonged to a large, burly man, whose great face was dominated by thick lips and a beak nose.

"A boy, Mr Jaggers," said Estella.

"A boy of the neighbourhood?"

"Yes, sir," I said.

"And how do you come to be here?"

"Miss Havisham sent for me, sir."

"Well, behave yourself. I have a pretty large experience of boys, and you're a bad set of fellows. So you mind out, and behave yourself."

With these words he disappeared, and I followed Estella on the route she had taken

before, until she left me with Miss Havisham.

"So, the days have worn away, have they?"

"Yes, ma'am. Today is —"

"I don't want to know! Are you ready to play?"

"I don't think I am, ma'am, I'm afraid."

"Since this house strikes you as old and grave, boy, and you are unwilling to play, perhaps you are willing to work?"

"Yes, ma'am."

"Then you may take me for a walk," she said, rising from her chair and offering me her arm. "Come on, walk me!"

I walked her round the room several times like an invalid, and then she gestured to me to open two tall doors. They led to a spacious, musty room, dominated by a long table laden with all kinds of dusty, cobweb-ridden things. Spiders, beetles and mice ran all over it, apparently unmoved by our entrance.

"This is where I shall be laid when I am dead," she said. "This is where they will come and look at me. What do you think that is, where those cobwebs are?"

"I can't guess what it is, ma'am."

"It's a great cake. A wedding cake. My wedding cake. Mine!"

She paused for a moment, staring at the appalling sight on the table.

"Today is my birthday, Pip, but I don't suffer it to be mentioned. On this day of the year, long before you were born, this heap of decay was brought here. It and I have worn away together. The mice have gnawed away at it, and sharper teeth than those of mice have gnawed away at me."

She suddenly looked tired, and sighed heavily. "When the ruin is complete, and when they lay me dead in my bride's dress on the bride's table, so much the better if it is done on this day of the year!"

She looked at the table as though in a dream, then turned to me. "Call Estella!"

We played cards as before, and I lost as before, and Estella treated me as before, though she did not speak. After half-a-dozen games, Miss Havisham said: "Estella, take Pip down for some lunch. I expect he would like to sit in the courtyard. Is there sun today?"

"Yes, ma'am," I replied. "It's a fine day."

"I'm sure it is. Now, Pip, you must come again in five days. Goodbye."

Estella left me sitting on a bench in the courtyard, and then returned with some lunch, once again putting it on the ground in front of me, before vanishing again. I was just about to eat when I was confronted by a pale, tall boy.

"Who let you in?" he asked.

"Miss Estella," I replied.

"I see. Let's go and fight!"

I have since often asked myself why I did what he said, but his manner was so final that I followed him as if under a spell. He led on a few paces, then took off his jacket.

"I ought to give you a reason for fighting, I suppose," he said, and then he butted my stomach with his head.

This both hurt and annoyed me, and I squared up to fight him. But I was quite frightened, for though of my own age he was taller than I and made a great show with his fists. "Laws of the game!" he declared, bobbing and weaving in front of me. "Regular rules!"

I have never been so surprised as when, after taking several weak punches from him, I let out the first real blow and saw him lying on his back, holding his cheek. He shaped up to me again, tapped me a few times, and then I knocked him

down again; and again; and again. Finally he stayed down, looking up at me through reddened eyes: "That means you've won!"

His spirit inspired me with great respect, and I felt no satisfaction in my victory.

"Can I help you?" I asked, offering my hand.

"No, thank you."

"Then — goodbye."

"The same to you."

When I reached the courtyard I found Estella with the keys, but instead of going towards the gate she stepped back near some bushes, and beckoned me to follow.

"Come here," she said. "You may kiss me if you like."

I kissed her cheek as she turned it to me. I would have gone through a good deal to kiss Estella — but I felt the kiss was given to the coarse boy as a piece of money might be given, and that it was worth nothing of any value.

On my next visit to Satis House I learned that I was expected to walk Miss Havisham round the two rooms she used for as much as three hours at a time. This I did on every visit I made there, which from now on was every other day.

We soon began to know each other a little better, and I told her of my desire to learn more. But she did not help me in this; indeed she seemed to prefer me to remain ignorant. I received nothing on all these occasions but my daily dinner.

Estella was always there, and always led me in and out. Sometimes she would coldly tolerate me; sometimes she would condescend to me;

sometimes she would tell me that she hated me; sometimes she would be quite familiar with me. But never again did she tell me I might kiss her.

We had fun, now and then. Miss Havisham quite took to a blacksmith's working song I sang once, and we would often sing it as we walked; even Estella joined in once or twice.

The only person who knew of all this was Biddy, to whom I told everything. I could not bring myself to tell Joe of my fight, and after that found it difficult to relate the details of the happenings at the big house — let alone my new feelings.

Discussions went on endlessly between my sister and Mr Pumblechook as to the outcome of these visits, but Joe took little part in them. His wife took this to mean that, since I was now old enough to be apprenticed to Joe, he was not favourable to my being taken away from the forge.

Then, one morning, nearly a year after my first visit to Satis House, Miss Havisham asked me to take Joe with me the next time; and so, after leaving Mrs Joe at Mr Pumblechook's house, I led a very nervous blacksmith, dressed in his Sunday best, to the strange house.

"I understand that you are the husband of Pip's sister," began Miss Havisham, "and that the boy is to be apprenticed to you. Is that so, Mr Gargery?"

Joe was almost too terrified to reply. "Yes, ma'am, that is, I mean to say, yes, he is."

"And does the boy have any objection."

"No, ma'am, not so far as I know. But if Pip had no heart for the life of a smithy, I wouldn't try to force my wishes on him."

"Well, Pip has been a good boy here and earned a premium. There are twenty-five guineas in this bag. Give it to your master, Pip."

Joe could hardly believe his ears and was almost speechless.

"Thank you, ma'am, thank you kindly. I — I don't know what to say."

"Am I to come again, Miss Havisham?" I asked.

"No, Gargery is your master now. Goodbye, Pip."

Estella spoke not a word as she led us out and locked the door behind us. Once outside, Joe leaned his back against the courtyard wall: "Astonishing, Pip. This is a-stonishing!" And he kept murmuring that, or something very like it, at intervals all the way back to Mr Pumblechook's house.

Once Mrs Joe and Mr Pumblechook had taken this news in, and the corn-chandler had wallowed in my sister's declarations of gratitude for introducing me to Miss Havisham, I was taken round to the town hall to have my indentures to J. Gargery signed by a magistrate. That evening, a little of the twenty-five guineas was spent on a dinner at the Blue Boar, but I could not bring myself to enjoy it, and felt like a commodity that had been bought at a sale.

At last, when I finally got to my little bedroom, I was truly wretched, and knew I should never like Joe's trade. I had liked the idea once, but once was not now. I had believed in the forge as the glowing road to manhood, but in a single year all that was changed. Now it seemed

coarse and common, and I saw a future of dull endurance set out for me. I knew my feelings were ungracious, even ungrateful, but I could not help them. I felt ashamed of my home and who I was.

Looking back now, I can see that I served my apprenticeship and never ran away not because I was faithful, but because Joe was faithful; and that I worked hard not because I saw virtue in it, but because Joe did. Any good that came from that apprenticeship came from Joe, and not from me.

Although I now no longer visited the school-room, I still had my special lessons from Biddy whenever I could; and, whenever I could, I tried to pass on my learning to Joe. One day, during one of these sessions, I suggested that I pay Miss Havisham a visit to thank her. Joe thought it a poor idea — he said Miss Havisham had been very final — but he nevertheless agreed to my taking a half-day holiday for the purpose.

My visit was short and far from sweet. A maid, not Estella, opened the gate, and Miss Havisham was quite sharp with me.

"Well, Pip," she said, "I hope you want nothing — for you'll get nothing."

"No, indeed, Miss Havisham. I only wanted you to know that I am doing well in my apprenticeship, and am always obliged to you."

"Come now and then, Pip. Yes, come on your birthday." She tapped her fingers on her dressing-table. "I see you're looking round for Estella. Well, she's abroad, educating for a lady, and far out of reach; prettier than ever and admired by all who see her. Do you feel you have lost her?"

There was unpleasant enjoyment in her voice, and she spared me the trouble of replying by curtly dismissing me; but the news of Estella had made me all the more dissatisfied with my lot.

On the way back through the town I met Joe, and we walked the four miles to the house together. Late in the afternoon we heard the gun of the prison-ship, warning of an escape, and my mind raced back to the encounters with my convict.

The house was quiet, and as we approached I had the sensation of something being wrong. We opened the door and there, on the kitchen floor, was Mrs Joe, her body lying in the strangest of positions. She was unconscious, knocked down, it seemed, by a severe blow to the back of her head.

The next few days are a blur to me — a confusion of doctors, constables and soldiers — as my sister lay helpless in bed, her speech gone, her hearing impaired, her memory damaged. She communicated her needs by feebly writing with chalk on a slate, but with her letters being so bad she was sometimes offered the wrong food and drink. We were at a loss to find suitable help for her until, following the death of Mr Worple's great aunt, Biddy came to look after her — and indeed to look after us.

Strangely, Mrs Joe was altogether a person of a different disposition now, patient and understanding, though every few weeks she would have a relapse and hold her head in her hands for hours on end, wailing dreadfully. It was during one of these bouts, some nine months after the attack, that my sister died.

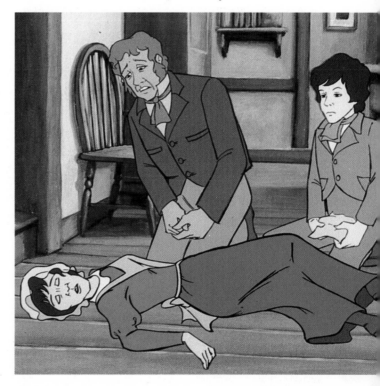

4 My Life is Changed

I now fell into a regular routine of apprentice life — a life which was varied only by the arrival of my birthday and another visit to Miss Havisham. The interview lasted but a few minutes, and she gave me a guinea; as I left she told me to come again on my next birthday, and this became an annual custom.

At home, Biddy was a very different housekeeper from Mrs Joe, and she found time to improve her learning a good deal. In the summer we used to go walking out on the marshes, and on one such occasion I told her of my feelings about my calling in life, and of my desire to be a gentleman. Biddy was, as usual, understanding and considerate — and she knew what had caused these feelings in me — but neither she nor I could see the remotest way I could even begin to bring about such a change in my fortunes.

Then, quite suddenly, in the third year of my apprenticeship to Joe, an event occurred which was indeed to change the course of my life.

Joe and I were working in the forge one bright morning when we had a visitor. He did not recognize me, but I certainly recognized him — as the man I had seen in the garden on my second visit to Satis House.

"Do I address Joe Gargery?" he began.

"You do," replied Joe, shutting off the bellows.

"And is this Pip, your apprentice?"

"It is. And could I ask your name, sir?"

"My name is Jaggers, and I am a lawyer in London — a pretty well-known lawyer. I have unusual business with you, and I will start by explaining that it is not of my creation. If my advice had been asked, I should not have been here. What I have to do as the confidential agent of another, I do; no less, no more."

Our visitor came up closer to us. "Now, Joseph Gargery, I am the bearer of an offer to relieve you of this young fellow. You would not object to cancel his indentures, at his request and for his good?"

"No, sir. Lord forbid that I should stand in Pip's way."

"Then the communication I have is that this young fellow has great expectations."

Joe and I gasped, and looked at one another.

"I am instructed to communicate to him," continued Mr Jaggers, talking to Joe but waving his fat finger sideways at me, "that he will come into a handsome property. Further, that it is the desire of the present owner of that property that he be immediately removed from this place and be brought up as a gentleman — in a word, as a young man of great expectations."

My dream was out; my wild fancy was sober reality: Miss Havisham was going to make my fortune on a grand scale.

"Now, Mr Pip, you are to understand, first, that it is the request of your benefactor that you will always bear the name 'Pip'. You are to understand, second, that the name of your benefactor remains a profound secret until that person chooses to reveal it, and that secret is held only by the person from whom you derive your expectations and myself. It is the intention of the person to reveal it at first hand to yourself, but where and when I cannot say; it may be years hence. You are to understand, third, that you are prohibited from making any mention or inquiry in this direction; if you have a suspicion in your breast as to the identity of your benefactor, you must keep it there. You will please consider me as your guardian. Now, do you object to any of these conditions?"

"No — no, sir," I stammered.

"I should think not. We come next to mere details of arrangement. You must know that although I use the term 'expectations' more than once, you are not endowed with expectations only. There is already in my possession a sum of money sufficient for your education and maintenance, and the way will be prepared for you. Now, when will you come to London? Shall we say a week from today?"

Mr Jaggers gave me twenty pounds to buy clothes and my ticket, as well as a card with his London address; but Joe, despite being pressed, refused to take any money for the loss of my services. The lawyer then left, leaving Joe and I stunned and speechless.

Both Joe and Biddy, though sad at the prospect of my going, were almost as pleased for me as I was for myself. The first chance that Biddy and I had to be alone, I suggested that she should help Joe in his learning and his manners, ready for the day when I was able to help him move on to a higher sphere of activity in life.

"Have you never considered that he may be proud?"

"Proud?" I replied.

"Yes. He may be too proud to let anyone take him out of a place he's competent to fill, and fills well and with respect. To tell the truth, I think he is, though you must know him far better than I do."

"I am very sorry to see this in you, Biddy. I did not expect it. You are envious, Biddy, and grudging. You are dissatisfied on account of my rise in fortune, and you can't help showing it."

"Whether you scold me or approve of me, Pip, you may depend on my trying to do all that lies in my power, here, at all times. And whatever opinion you take away of me, it shall make no difference to my remembrance of you. Yet a gentleman should not be unjust."

When I went into the town to buy my new clothes a few days later I called on Mr Pumblechook, and he could not have been more obliging. He congratulated both of us in equal measure for my good fortune, and wined and dined me as though I were already a man of fortune.

I then made my way to see Miss Havisham.

"Well, Pip," she said curtly, "and what brings you here away from your birthday?"

"I start for London tomorrow, Miss Havisham," I replied, choosing my words with care, "and I thought you would not mind my taking leave of you. I have come into much good fortune since I saw you last, and I am very grateful for it."

"Yes, yes, I have seen Mr Jaggers. I have heard about it. So you are adopted by a rich person, not named, and Mr Jaggers is your guardian?"

"Yes, Miss Havisham."

"Well, you have a promising career before you. Be good — deserve it — and abide by Mr Jaggers' instructions. Goodbye, Pip."

She stretched out her hand, and I put it to my lips; and then I left my fairy godmother.

The coach was to stop at six o'clock the next morning on its way to London. The parting from Biddy and Joe was sad and tearful, but soon I could think of nothing but the exciting times that lay before me.

I was frightened at first by the great size of London, but I was also disappointed, for it was for the most part ugly, crooked, narrow and dirty. Mr Jaggers' office was near Smithfield, and there he told me of the arrangements that had been made on my behalf. I was to go to the rooms of one Herbert Pocket, son of Mr Matthew Pocket — whose name I had heard mentioned in conversations between Miss Havisham and Estella, and who was now to be my tutor.

The house I was to occupy off Chancery Lane was hardly what I had expected for a person of

my new standing, and I felt a sense of being cheated as I climbed the broken staircase to a dark landing and the door marked *Mr Pocket, Junior*. My concern about the surroundings vanished when the tenant opened the door to greet me — for Mr Pocket, Junior turned out to be none other than the pale young gentleman I had fought with in the gardens of Satis House!

"The idea of it being *you*," he said.

"And the idea of it being *you*," I replied.

"I do hope you will forgive me for knocking you about so dreadfully."

At this we both burst out laughing, and he invited me inside. He showed me around the rooms, and when we had a cup of tea I asked Herbert what he had been doing at Miss Havisham's house that day.

"Miss Havisham had sent for me," he began, "to see if she could take a fancy to me. But she couldn't — or rather, she didn't. If I had come out of it successfully, I suppose I should I have been provided for. Perhaps I should have been engaged to Estella."

"How did you bear such disappointment."

"I didn't care much for the idea, Pip. That girl's hard and haughty and capricious, and has been brought up by Miss Havisham to wreak revenge on all the male sex."

"Why?" I asked. "What revenge?"

"Lord, Pip! Don't you know? Well, it's quite a story — and it shall be saved until dinner."

Meantime, Herbert explained that he had been asked by his father, on behalf of Mr Jaggers, to take me in on my arrival in London; and that if things worked out well, this arrangement could become permanent. He said that my guardian was Miss Havisham's man of business and solicitor, and ran all her affairs.

Herbert Pocket had a frank and easy way with him that was very engaging, and I soon felt him to be a friend. He was amiable and cheerful, yet his figure was a little ungainly, and he was still very much the pale young gentleman.

I was burning with curiosity about the story of Miss Havisham when we sat down to dinner — a meal furnished entirely from the local coffee-house — but before he could start Herbert was forced to point out that it was not the custom for

young gentlemen to put their knife in their mouth — as I was about to do. Indeed it is worth noting here that throughout this meal — and throughout the first months of our subsequent times together — he constantly educated me in the correct ways of all kinds of social manners; and that he did so in such a friendly and endearing fashion that neither of us ever felt even slightly embarrassed by the process.

"Now," he said, taking a deep breath, "Miss Havisham was a spoilt child, as you must know. Her mother died when she was young, and her father denied her nothing. Her father was a country gentleman, and a brewer, down in your part of the country. He was very rich and very proud — and so was his daughter.

"When he died, Miss Havisham was in her youth, and she now became an heiress. She was seen as a great match, and attracted many proposals of marriage. Now, there appeared on the scene — at the races, at the balls, at the parties, anywhere you like — a certain man, who courted Miss Havisham and made love to her. He professed to be devoted to her, and there is no doubt that she perfectly idolized him. The wedding was arranged, and the great day came. But not the bridegroom. He wrote a letter —"

"Which she received when she was dressing for her marriage?" I interrupted. "At twenty minutes to nine?"

"The very hour and minute," continued Herbert, nodding, "at which she stopped all the clocks in the place. When she recovered from a bad illness she laid the whole place waste, as you have seen it, and she has never since looked upon the light of day."

"Who was this man who broke her heart?"

"A trickster, a gambler and a cheat."

"So why didn't he marry her and come into all the property?"

"I don't know, Pip. He had got his hands on a good deal of her money before that day, and perhaps he was married already."

"Do you know what happened to him?"

Herbert shrugged his shoulders. "Not exactly. I believe he fell into deeper shame and ruin, and there were stories that he had gone to prison."

"And Estella was adopted?"

"Yes, and brought up to hate men. There has always been an Estella, ever since I have heard of Miss Havisham, but I know no more. Now, there is a perfectly open understanding between us. All I know about Miss Havisham, you know."

"And all I know," I replied, "you know."

"Good. So there can be no competition between us. As to the condition that you may not inquire or discuss the identity of your benefactor — you may be very sure that it will be never be touched upon, or even approached, by me or anyone belonging to me."

And so, for the present, the subject of Miss Havisham and Estella was closed.

Herbert worked in the City of London, at a company insuring ships and their cargoes. But he was quick to tell me of his plans to one day be a shipper of all kinds of exotic goods himself. There came on me, however, the strong impression that Mr Pocket, Junior would never be rich and successful, and that he would always endure his own strange kind of well-to-do poverty.

The two of us got along famously, and over the next few days he introduced me to the life of London: to the theatre, to the drinking clubs, to the restaurants, to the great buildings, to the royal parks, and to the river — with which I fell so much in love that I later bought a rowing boat. And all the time, I learned from him the essentials of being a gentleman.

On the first Sunday we went to visit his family's home in Hammersmith — a large family of seven children, living in a large house with two young gentleman lodgers — and Mr Pocket, Senior informed me he had been asked to be my tutor. No particular training or occupation was intended: simply an accumulation of knowledge on all relevant things. Thus while Herbert Pocket was to improve my manners, his father was to improve my mind, and a weekly schedule was arranged for this purpose.

The following Monday I went to see Mr Jaggers to tell him of these arrangements, and discovered that I had only to ask for money and it would be provided there and then by his clerk. As a result I soon contracted expensive habits, and began to spend an amount of money that a few short months before I should have thought almost fabulous. Thus began my life of a young gentleman in London.

5 Returns from Abroad

Several months of this carefree existence had passed when I received a letter from Biddy, informing me that Joe was to visit me the following day on a matter of importance. I was filled with dread, for I was already part of a different world, and the distance between Joe's marshlands and the crowded streets of London seemed almost too great to bridge.

Unfortunately Herbert was at home when he arrived in his Sunday best, and I found Joe's crude ways and humble manners — he called me 'sir' — irritating and embarrassing. He had, it appeared, been approached by his uncle Mr Pumblechook on behalf of Miss Havisham; she wished me to visit Satis House and see Estella, who had returned from France. Quite why the message had come this strange route I never did discover — Miss Havisham could have written to Mr Jaggers, or Biddy could have conveyed the message in her letter — but in any case I was only too delighted with the invitation, and set out the next day for Satis House.

In the coach I pondered the reason for this journey, and on Miss Havisham's plans for me. She had adopted Estella, and she had as good as adopted me, and it could not fail to be her intention to bring us together. It must be for me to restore the desolate house, admit the sunlight into the dark rooms and set the clocks going — to do all the shining deeds of the young knight of romance, and marry the princess.

I was let in at the gate by a servant I had not seen before, and found my way to Miss Havisham's door.

"Pip's rap," I heard her say. "Come in, Pip!"

She was sitting in front of the dressing-table, as unchanged as ever. "Well?"

"I heard, Miss Havisham, that you were so kind as to wish me to come and see you, and I came directly."

"Well, you are quite the young gentleman now, Pip. You have obviously made good use of your fortune."

I was about to reply when the door opened and in walked a captivating young woman. It was Estella, as distant and divine as ever.

"Do you find her much changed, Pip?" asked Miss Havisham, with her greedy look.

"At first I did. But now I can see the old Estella, and it's a beautiful sight to behold."

"What! Come now, Pip, you found the old Estella proud and insulting. Don't you remember?"

"Yes, Miss Havisham, but —"

"Is *he* changed, my dear?" she cut in, talking to Estella.

"Very much," said Estella, looking at me.

"Less coarse and common?" inquired Miss Havisham, laughing.

Estella nodded, and laughed too. She treated me as a boy still, but lured me on.

"You've both changed, which is as it should be. But I have not. Nothing has changed here. Now, Estella, I would like a word with Pip."

As soon as Estella had left us, Miss Havisham turned on me. "Is she beautiful, graceful, well-grown? Do you admire her?"

"Everybody must who sees her, Miss Havisham."

"Love her, Pip, love her!" she whispered, grabbing my hand. "If she favours you, love her! If she wounds you, love her! If she tears your heart to pieces — and as it gets older and stronger it will tear deeper — love her, love her, *love her*!"

Never had I seen such passionate eagerness as was joined to the utterance of these words, yet she then suddenly let go of me and resumed her usual poise. "Estella is going to live with friends of mine in Richmond for a time, Pip, and I want you to accompany her there on the coach tomorrow, and see to it that no harm comes to her."

I said I would be only too happy to do so, and, no more being said on the subject, I took my leave. I stayed at the Blue Boar Inn in the town, excusing myself from visiting Joe and Biddy on the grounds of limited time.

On the coach the next morning, Estella and I talked of her schooling in France and my life in London and my friendship with Herbert, but

then I reminded her of our childhood — of her games, her taunts, and her kiss. She was proud and haughty still, but even more lovely, and I said so.

"Pip," she said, with a cold, careless smile, "will you never take warning?"

"Of what?"

"Of me."

"Warning not to be attracted by you, do you mean?"

"You silly boy. How can you talk such nonsense? You must know that I have no heart; no feelings, no sentiment. If you don't know what I mean, you are blind. I have not bestowed my affections elsewhere for I have none to bestow. And if we are to be thrown much together, you had better believe it at once."

I could and would not believe it. I loved her, adored her. But though she was now to live in Richmond, less than half-a-day's journey from my rooms, she may as well have been a thousand miles away.

Herbert seemed not in the least surprised when I told him of my feelings for Estella, and said that he had always known it; but he did, in the gentlest way, suggest that I abandon the cause, for she had all the faults of Miss Havisham. I would have none of it, and never gave up hope of winning her love.

I visited Estella several times in Richmond, but I always left with the peculiar impression that although I thought I would be happy with her, I was never happy when I *was* with her. She showed no signs of melting towards me — or towards any other as far as I could see, though she was greatly admired by many — and she still teased me mercilessly at times.

I soon settled back into my old life in London which, though for the most part enjoyable, was punctuated with bouts of boredom. The influences of my expectations in me were, I was aware, not all good; nor were they all beneficial to Herbert, since my lavish habits led his easy nature into expenses he could not afford.

We spent as much money as we could, but we were always more or less miserable, as most of our acquaintances were. There was a fiction among us that we were constantly enjoying ourselves, and a dark truth that we never really did.

I was always uneasy, too, about my behaviour towards Joe and Biddy. Sometimes I thought I should have been happier had I never seen Miss Havisham's face, and risen to manhood content to be partners with Joe in the old forge. But the longer I left it, the more difficult it became to do anything about it.

It was while I was in this melancholy frame of mind that I reached my twenty-first birthday — some eight months after Herbert had come of age — and I was asked by Mr Jaggers to visit his office. My guardian informed me, in disapproving tones, that he knew I was in debt, and handed me a note for five hundred pounds.

"Now that handsome sum of money is your own, in earnest of your expectations," he explained. "And you are to live at that rate, drawing one hundred and twenty-five pounds a quarter from my clerk, until your benefactor is revealed. As I have told you before, I am the mere agent. I execute my instructions, and am paid for doing so. I think them unwise, but I am not paid for giving any opinion on their merits."

Unknown to Mr Jaggers, I arranged through devious means over the next few weeks for money brokers to put one half of my gift Herbert's way, but the whole business was so cleverly managed that he had not the least suspicion that my hand was in it.

Some five or six months after my coming of age I returned to my rooms one wet night from dinner at a friend's house. Herbert was away in France on business for his firm and I climbed the stairs slowly, for I was not in a gay mood.

As I lowered my candle to put the key in the door, there was a sudden sound behind me, and then a voice.

"Mr Pip?"

I turned to see a large figure in the shadows on the landing, and I moved my lamp towards its face. I could see it was a man about sixty, hardened by exposure to the weather, and with a sinister patch over one eye.

"That is my name," I replied. "What is your business?"

"My business? Ah, yes, I will explain my business, by your leave."

"Do you wish to come in?"

"Yes, but there's no-one near, is there? No-one came with you, nor no-one inside?"

"Why do you, a stranger coming to my rooms at night, ask such a question?"

"Oh, you're a game one, that's for sure. I'm glad you've growed up a game one!"

Then I knew him! I could not recall a single feature, but I knew him! If the wind and the rain had driven away the intervening years, and swept us to the churchyard where we stood face to face, I could not have known my convict more distinctly than I knew him now.

"I think you had better come in." I said it calmly, though I was confused and shaken.

Once inside, and with the lamps lit, he took my hands, raised them to his lips, and kissed them. "You acted noble, my boy! Noble, Pip. And I've never forgot it!"

"If you have come here to thank me, it was not necessary," I said, taking away my hands. "Still, however you have found me out, there must be something good in the feeling that has brought you here. I am glad you have repented and recovered yourself, and I am glad you have come to thank me. But you must understand that I cannot wish to renew that chance intercourse with you of long ago, under these different circumstances."

He said nothing, but gazed at me with a slight smile.

"You are wet, and look weary. Will you drink something before you go."

He nodded, and I made him some hot rum and water. When he put it to his lips, I saw with amazement that he was weeping.

"I hope you do not think I spoke harshly to you just now. I had no intention of doing it, and I am sorry for it if I did. I wish you well, and happy."

He stretched out his hand to me, and I gave

him mine. Then I beckoned him to sit down.

"How are you living?" I asked.

"I've been a sheep-farmer, stock-breeder and other trades besides, many a thousand mile of stormy water from this."

"I hope you have done well."

"I've done wonderful well, Pip. I'm famous for it. But may I make so bold as to ask you how come you have done so well, since you and me was out on them shivering marshes?"

I told him, briefly, the story of how I had been chosen to succeed to some property.

At this point my visitor began asking a long series of leading questions about my life, though none required an answer and none was given. He knew every detail of my arrangements, to the last letter and penny, and the truth of my position gradually came upon me. I could not have spoken one word then, though it had been to save my life.

"Yes, Pip, dear boy, I've made a gentleman of you! It's *me* what has done it! I swore that time, sure as ever I earned a guinea, that guinea would go to you. I lived rough so that you should live smooth. I worked hard so that you should be above work. That hunted dog what you kept alive got his head so high that he could make a gentleman — and Pip, you're him!"

The dread I had of this man, and the distaste I felt for him, could not have been exceeded if he had been some terrible beast.

"Look'ee here, Pip. I'm your second father. You're my son — more to me than any son. I've put away money, only for you to spend. When I was a hired-out shepherd in a lonely hut, not seeing no faces but faces of sheep till I half forgot what men's and women's faces was like, I see *your* face. And each time I says to myself, 'If I get liberty and money, I'll make that boy a gentleman.' And I done it!"

Again he took my hand and shook it, while my blood ran cold within me.

"Don't mind me talking, Pip, for you ain't looked slowly forward to this as I have. You wasn't prepared for this, as I was, I know that. But didn't you never think it might be me?"

"No, no," I replied. "Never!"

"Well, it was me, and single-handed. Not a soul in it but me and Mr Jaggers."

Oh, if that man had never come; if only he had left me at the forge — far from contented, yet by comparison so happy.

He took another great gulp of his drink. "When I was rich, I says to myself, 'If I ain't a gentleman, and got no learning, I'm the owner of such.' That's the way I kept myself going. I knew I would come for certain one day, and make myself known to you, on your own ground."

I tried to collect my thoughts, but I was still stunned.

"Where will you put me, dear boy? I must be put somewheres."

"You mean — to sleep?"

"Yes, and to sleep long and sound, for I've been tossed and washed by the sea for months."

"My friend is absent. You must — you must have his room."

Suddenly he stood over me, pointing his finger at my face. "Look'ee here, Pip. Caution is necessary."

"How do you mean — caution?"

"I was sent to Australia for life. I'm a free man there, for I won my pardon, but it's death to come back. I should be hanged for certain if I was took in England."

Nothing was needed but this. The wretched man, after loading me with his gold and silver for years, had risked his life to come to me, and I held it there, in my keeping. I explained that Herbert was not expected back for two more days, and that we would consider the best plan to follow in the morning.

When he had finally gone to bed — a pistol laying beside him on his pillow — I sat for hours in the drawing-room, trying to sort all this out in my swirling mind.

My first thoughts were of my ficticious benefactor. Miss Havisham's intentions towards me were all a mere dream! Estella was not designed for me; I was suffered at Satis House only as a convenience, a model to practise on when no other model was at hand.

But this was not the sharpest pain. That came when I realized that it was for a convict, a man whose crimes I did not know but who could be now taken from my rooms and hanged, that I had deserted Joe. I would not have gone back to Joe now, nor Biddy, for any consideration, because of my own worthless conduct. And I could never, never undo what I had done.

6 Fire and Water

My first concern the next morning was to invent an identity for my unwelcome guest, and as he devoured breakfast I explained that I would say he was my uncle. His name, it turned out, was Abel Magwitch, but on the prison-ship he had taken the name Provis, and we decided to stay with that. I also resolved to keep him in my rooms until Herbert returned and lodgings could be arranged.

That first afternoon I went to see Mr Jaggers, who of course knew of my visitor. He said he had counselled Magwitch against returning to England when he had written asking for my address, but he had been determined to come. Jaggers knew, too, that I had always believed Miss Havisham to be my benefactor, but he claimed, with ample justification, that he had never said nor done anything to encourage me in that mistaken belief.

The two days until Herbert's return seemed an age, particularly since we could go out only late at night and I was thus imprisoned with Provis for hour after hour. Dear Herbert was sworn to secrecy before being told the mysterious tale, and he obviously shared both my shock and my distaste for our visitor. His advice was to not forsake him, since he might become desperate and dangerous, but to work towards the goal of smuggling him out of the country.

That evening, having secured suitably discreet lodgings for Provis nearby in Essex Street, we asked him about his life — and especially with reference to the man on the marshes that cold Christmas Day. It was a long, sad story of struggle and cruelty and imprisonment, and I shall relate here only the chapter that touches directly on this other party.

"A matter of over twenty year ago," he began, taking a gulp of rum, "I got acquainted with a man whose skull I'd crack open now if ever I saw him. His right name was Compeyson, and that's the man, dear Pip, you saw me pounding in the ditch. He set up to be a gentleman, this Compeyson, and he had learning. He was a smooth one to talk to, and a dab hand at the ways of gentlefolks. He was good looking, too, and had a way with the women, though he were married.

" 'To judge from appearances, you're out of luck,' he says to me. 'Perhaps yours is going to change.' Well, Compeyson took me on to be his man and partner. But his business turns out to be swindling, forging, passing stolen money and such like. That man got me into such straits as

made me his black slave. I was always in debt to him, always under his thumb, always in danger for him. He'd no more heart than a lump of iron. He was as cold as death.

"At last he tried his tricks once too often, passing a forged note to a jeweller, and he was arrested in the street. And I was arrested after he told them where I was. At the trial he used his charms and educated ways on the judge, and blamed me for his troubles. And when we're sentenced, he gets seven years and I gets fourteen. I vowed then I'd do him for what he'd done to me.

"So on the prison-ship I got him a good one. I only gave him a scar, before they pulled me off, but I would have killed him if I could. Then I escaped — and he escaped too — and you saw, Pip, how I nearly killed him.

"Of course he had much the best of it to the last — his character was so good. He had escaped when he was made half wild by me and by my murderous intentions, and his punishment was light. But I was put in irons, brought to trial again and sent for life. But I didn't stay for life, for I won my pardon fair and square."

He wiped his brow with his handkerchief, and took another drink.

"Is he dead?" I asked.

"He hopes *I* am, if he's alive, you can be sure of that. I never heard no more of him."

Herbert was now writing with his pencil in the cover of a book. He pushed it over to me, as Provis gazed into the fire. I read: *Compeyson is the man who professed to be Miss Havisham's lover.*

I shut the book and nodded slightly to my friend, and put the book aside. We said nothing, but both looked at Provis as he stood smoking by the fire.

Neither Herbert nor I doubted the consequences if Compeyson were alive and should discover our secret. But we resolved not to mention anything about our plans for Provis — he seemed quite set on staying in England, despite the dangers — until I had made an important visit.

There was an air of utter loneliness at Satis House now, and though everything inside was unchanged, Miss Havisham seemed even more desolate than before.

"And what wind blows you here, Pip?" she inquired as I entered her morbid room.

"I have found out who my patron is, Miss Havisham. It is not a fortunate discovery, and is not likely to enrich me in reputation or fortune. There are reasons why I must say no more of that. It is not my secret, but another's."

"Well?"

"When you brought me here as a boy it was to torture me with Estella, wasn't it?"

"No, no, I —"

"And when I fell into the mistake I have so long remained in, you led me on."

"I *let* you *go* on, Pip. But you made your own snares. *I* never made them for you."

I knew it to be true. She was right about my folly, just as Jaggers had been right. I had

deluded myself, and it was senseless to blame others.

"Oh, Miss Havisham, there have been sore mistakes. My life has been a blind and thankless one. I want forgiveness and direction far too much to be bitter with you."

She turned her face to me for the first time since I had come in, and took both my hands in hers, and drew me to her, and began sobbing. "What have I done!" she cried. "What have I done!"

"If you mean what have you done to injure me, then the answer is very little. I should have loved Estella under any circumstances."

"I know, Pip, I know that. And now she is married to a cruel man."

I had been aware for some time that Estella was engaged, but these words still came as a shock, and served only to increase my misery — and hers.

"What have I done!" she repeated. "O, Pip, what have I done!" She wrung her hands, and clutched her head, and returned to this cry over and over again.

There was nothing more to be said. I left her, weeping, standing now by the fire, and made my way slowly downstairs. I had just reached the light of the courtyard when I heard a piercing scream from her room, and then another, longer one. I dashed back up the dark stairs, flung open the door and saw her running towards me, shrieking, a whirl of blazing flame all about her.

I snatched off my coat and smothered her with it, throwing her to the floor and dousing the flames on her writhing body. Then I grabbed the great cloth from the table, and with it dragged down the heap of ugly things that lay on it. We were on the floor struggling like desperate enemies, and it seemed that the closer I covered her, the more wildly she shrieked and tried to free herself. At last, as the black shower of her burnt dress fell around us, she lay still.

Assistance was sent for, and it was pronounced that her injuries, though serious, were far from hopeless; the main danger lay in the nervous shock. I stayed with her until the next day, until all worry was past (and to have my own singed hands dressed); then I attended to all the necessary details of such circumstances, including a letter to Estella. As I could then be of no further service, and had pressing reasons for leaving, I set out for London.

It became apparent soon after my return that Provis' presence in London was hardly a secret. Indeed from a network of sources — notably Mr Jaggers' clerk, with whom I had always been on excellent terms and who now reported on the news travelling around Newgate Prison — it was concluded not only that our movements were being closely watched, but that it was almost certain that the spy was none other than Compeyson.

We decided that Provis should lie low in a house down by the river at Limehouse, one belonging to the father of Herbert's fiancé, Clara. While well off my usual beat, Herbert was a frequent visitor and would act as messenger. The house was also well placed to slip our man on board a packet ship on the river.

Provis, who occupied the two cabin rooms at the top of the house, took all this in his stride and was reasonable throughout, though I stopped

short of informing him that the menace was Compeyson. His return was a venture, he said, and he had always known it to be a risky one. He would do nothing to make it more dangerous, and had little fear of his safety with such good help.

Herbert suggested that I move my boat from Hammersmith down to Blackfriars, and that we should be seen rowing regularly so that suspicions would not be aroused when the day came. Both Provis and I liked this scheme, and with everything arranged I rose to go, taking half an hour's start of Herbert.

"I don't like to leave you here," I said to Provis, "though I cannot doubt you are safer here than near me. Goodbye."

"Dear Pip," he said, clasping my hands. "I don't know when we will meet again, and I don't like goodbye. Say 'goodnight'."

"Goodnight. When the time comes you may be certain I shall be ready. Goodnight!"

The man's dignity in the circumstances, and his great trust in us, caused a change in my opinion of him, and over the next weeks I found, through Herbert, that he was, without losing my pity, gaining my respect.

We set to work the next week, though my hands were still a little painful. Sometimes I would go out alone, sometimes with Herbert;

and gradually the distance was extended, first past London Bridge and then, after some weeks, all the way down to the estuary at Erith. Though we heard no more information to alarm us, I could not get rid of the notion of being watched. Once felt, it is a haunting idea, and impossible to shake off.

My worldly affairs were now rather gloomy, and I was pressed for money by more than one creditor. Even I began to know the want of ready money in my pocket, but I had determined that

it would be a heartless fraud to take any more money from my benefactor.

After months of waiting and preparation, the day for our deed was finally set. Herbert had discovered two likely ships, the first leaving for Hamburg at six o'clock, the second bound for Antwerp at a quarter past that hour. If we failed to hail the first, there was always another chance of success with the second.

It was a cool but not unpleasant March night as Herbert and I set out from Blackfriars, I rowing and Herbert steering. Quietly we made our way to downstream to the Mill Pond Steps at Limehouse and there, as arranged, stood our cargo. We touched the jetty for a moment and he was aboard.

"Dear boy," he said, putting his hand on my shoulder as he took his seat. "Well done! Thank'ee."

Soon we were among the ships and the barges and the buoys, and we rowed within feet of both our vessels for a close look. Our plan was to run with the tide down to the long reaches below Gravesend, between Kent and Essex, where the estuary is broad and solitary, and choose a suitable resting-place until the arrival of the ships we intended to board.

The plan worked, but the two hours until the Hamburg boat came into view seemed like two days. We rowed quickly towards its channel, and then I stood up, waving my arms and shouting, "Passenger! Passenger!" for all I was worth. It was almost upon us before the paddles stopped churning, and it slowed to a halt.

Provis stood up and I took his hand. I told him how grieved I was that he should have risked so much for my sake.

"Dear boy, I've been content to take my chances. I've seen my boy — and he can be a gentleman now, with or without my help. Goodbye, Pip."

"Goodbye, and good luck."

There was no time for more, for the crew on the Hamburg ship threw down a ladder and a rope. Provis quickly shook hands with Herbert and thanked him heartily. Then one of the crew pointed to the bank, and shouted something to us in a language we did not understand. We all looked round — and there, heading towards us at a furious rate, was a Customs galley with uniformed officers and a passenger.

The sergeant at its bow shouted at us as he approached: "You have a returned transport there! His name is Abel Magwitch, otherwise Provis! I call on that man to surrender, and on you to assist!"

By now the Customs boat was almost on us, and there was no escape. Our cause was helpless. The sergeant continued to shout to us, and to the crew of the ship, when suddenly I recognized the man cringing in his galley.

Provis recognized him, too, and in a moment he was turned again into the beast I had encountered in the churchyard on the marshes.

"Compeyson!"

He dived headlong at the informer, and both

wretched men and women to be sentenced that dull April day, but in view of his exploits the judge paid special attention to him as he sat motionless in the crowded dock. The appointed punishment was death, and he was told he must prepare himself to die.

I earnestly hoped and prayed that he may die before the day of the hanging, but in the dread of his lingering on I wrote petitions to the Home Secretary and others in authority, setting forth my knowledge of him and explaining how it was that he had come back for my sake.

On the tenth day after the trial, and on my tenth visit, I found him in more discomfort than ever before, and his face was placid and ghostly.

"Are you in much pain today?"

"I don't complain of none, dear boy."

"You never do complain."

"Thank'ee, Pip, thank'ee. God bless you. You've never deserted me. God bless you — always."

He had spoken his last words. He smiled, and raised my hand to his lips. Then he gently let it sink again, with his own hands lying on it. The placid look came back, and passed away, and his head dropped on his still breast.

men crashed into the water. For a minute, maybe more, we could make out nothing; but then, some way off, Provis broke the surface, gasping for air. He swam, slowly, to the Customs galley, and they dragged him on board. Breathing fast and heavy, he collapsed in the bottom of the boat, clutching his side.

I knelt over him, from our boat, and he turned his head towards me. "I — I got 'im, young Pip," he said in a whisper. "At last — I got 'im!"

They put irons round my convict's legs, and rowed him to prison. I was allowed to go with him, for he was badly hurt, and as I sat there by his side, I felt that this was my rightful place while he still lived. My repugnance to him had all melted away, and I saw now only a man who had meant to be my benefactor, and who had felt affectionately, gratefully and generously towards me over many years.

He lay in the prison hospital very ill for the three weeks until the trial. He had broken two ribs, which had punctured a lung, and his breathing grew worse with every day.

The trial was short and clear, for nothing could deny the fact that he had returned to England, and it was impossible to do otherwise than find him guilty. He was one of thirty-two

Epilogue

Within days of my convict's death I fell ill, and with Herbert married and gone to live in Egypt, I was very much alone. This illness soon developed into a delirious fever, and I imagined on several occasions that I saw Joe's face in my ravings. It was not until I was stable again, some weeks later, that I realized it *was* Joe — dear, kind, forgiving Joe. I was a child again in his care, and he nursed me back to health.

One morning, I woke to find him gone. He had left a simple note — Biddy had taught him to read and write! — and enclosed was a receipt for my debts. Until then I had always supposed that my creditors had suspended their proceedings because of my illness; but the receipt was in Joe's name, and the blacksmith had paid my debts in full.

I determined to follow Joe to the forge, to thank him. But that wasn't my main purpose: that was to see dear Biddy, and ask her to go through life with me. So, three days later, I set off for the marsh country once again.

I put up at the Blue Boar, but my stay was blighted by the presence at dinner of Mr Pumblechook. He laid into me about my ingratitude — I had not been to visit his nephew nor him once all these years — and about fate now dealing me the blows I merited.

I was still pondering his outburst when I arrived at the forge. There I found Biddy, and Joe; they were arm in arm at the door of the house, as two youngsters who were in love. And indeed they were — and to be married the very next week.

I have often thought since how thankful we should all be that I had never breathed a word of my last pathetic hope to Joe. They deserved each other, and were so happy; and I was so pleased for both their sakes, if not for mine.

I sold all I had, and put aside as much as I could, and went out to join Herbert. When the matter of Egypt had first come up, shortly after the capture of my 'uncle', Herbert and Clara had entreated me to go to them, for a trial period if necessary, since he could offer me the position of clerk.

Many a year went round before I gained an interest in the business, but I lived happily with the Pockets, and maintained a constant correspondence with Joe and Biddy. We were not in a grand way of business, but we had a good name, and worked hard for our profits.

I had not seen Joe nor Biddy for eleven years when, one evening in October, I laid my hand on the latch of the old kitchen door — so softly that I was not heard, and I looked in unseen. There, smoking his pipe in the old place by the firelight, sat Joe; and there, fenced into the corner with Joe's leg, and sitting on my own stool looking at the fire, was — me!

Joe explained they had given him the name of Pip for my sake, and had hoped he might grow a little bit like me — and thought he had. I thought he had, too, and was flattered. I took the boy out for a walk the next morning, up to the churchyard, and when I perched him on a certain tombstone, he showed me which grave was sacred to the memory of Philip Pirrip, late of this parish.

When Biddy gently brought up the subject of Estella, I knew I should have to go up to Satis House one last time. Joe had told me when he had been my nurse that Miss Havisham was dead, and that Estella had received most of the estate, and shortly afterwards the house had been put up for auction.

I had heard since of Estella as leading an unhappy life, soon separated from her cruel and mean husband. I had heard of his death, too, from a riding accident, but for two years, I had heard nothing more.

There was no house now, and no brewery — just the old walled garden, overgrown and desolate. I had been in the courtyard only moments when I glimpsed a woman, and she saw me. It was Estella.

We talked of our melancholy past, and a new bond sprang up between us. I took her hand in mine, and we left the ruined place; and, just as the morning mists had risen long ago when I first left the forge, so the evening mists were rising now, and in all the broad expanse of tranquil light they showed to me, I saw no shadow of another parting from her.